Anyone But Me

for Ian B.

Library of Congress Catalog Card Number: 2002102949

ISBN 0-448-42653-6   2006 Printing

Anyone But Me

by Nancy Krulik • illustrated by John & Wendy

Grosset & Dunlap

Chapter 1

"I've got it! I've got it!"

The football soared right towards Katie Carew. She ran towards the ball, reached out her hands and . . . *oomph!* She missed it completely.

"You took your eyes off it again," Katie's best friend, Jeremy Fox, said, jogging up to her. He pushed his thin wire glasses higher up on his nose and ran his hands through his curly brown hair.

"I know," Katie replied simply. What else could she say?

"Katie, I can't believe you did that!" Kevin Camilleri shouted across the field. "You lost the whole game for us."

Just then George Brennan came charging across the field. He had a big smile on his face. Katie groaned. Of course George was happy. His team had just won the game— thanks to Katie's fumble!

"Don't yell at the secret weapon," George told Kevin.

"Secret weapon? Are you kidding?" Kevin asked. "Secret weapons help *win* games, George."

"Exactly," George agreed. "Katie's the secret weapon for *our* team!"

Katie blinked her eyes tight. She didn't want George to see her cry.

"Forget about George," Jeremy whispered to Katie. "He can't help being mean. He was just born that way."

Katie tried to smile. "Could be," she said.

The truth was, Katie wasn't really sure why George was nasty to everyone in class 3A. Most new kids tried to make friends. Not

George. He tried to make enemies.

Just then, Katie's other best friend,
Suzanne Lock, ran across the playground to
them. "Let's go play on the monkey bars for a
while," she suggested, pulling Katie and
Jeremy away from George. "I'll bet I can hang
upside down longer than either of you."

Katie stared at Suzanne. Her friend was
wearing a skirt! "You're going to turn upside
down in *that*?" Katie asked.

"Sure!" Suzanne said, yanking her skirt up to her bellybutton.

Katie's mouth flew open.

Jeremy blushed.

"It's okay, you guys," Suzanne laughed. "See, I'm wearing shorts under here. This way I can wear a skirt and still play."

Katie laughed. Leave it to Suzanne to find a way to look pretty and still hang upside down on the jungle gym.

"Okay! Last one at the monkey bars is a rotten egg," Katie called as she dashed away.

Suzanne and Jeremy took off after Katie. Katie held on to her lead, but not for long. Jeremy was the fastest runner in the class. He quickly pulled up next to Katie. Katie took a deep breath. She moved her feet faster than ever. But not fast enough. Jeremy zoomed into the lead.

Katie frowned. Well, at least she was ahead of Suzanne. Katie turned her head to see just how far behind Suzanne was and . . .

Splat!

Katie stepped right into a big, wet puddle. Gushy brown mud splashed all over her. Katie stopped running and looked down at her jeans.

"Oh, no!" she cried out. "What a mess!"

Katie wasn't kidding. She was a total mess. There were mud splatters all over her jeans. Her *favorite* jeans—the ones with the pink and blue flowers embroidered all over them.

If this were first grade, Katie could have changed into the clean clothes in her cubby. But Katie was in third grade now. Nobody in third grade kept a change of clothes at school. That was for babies. Katie was going to have to wear her mud-stained jeans for the whole rest of the day.

"Nice one, Carew," George shouted across the yard. "Check it out, everybody! There's a Mud Monster in the playground."

George stuck his arms straight out and walked around the yard pretending to be Frankenstein. The other kids laughed.

Katie wanted to cry. This was the worst recess ever. She wished Mrs. Derkman would blow her whistle and make everyone go in to class. Even doing schoolwork had to be better than this!

"George, go away or I'm gonna tell," Suzanne warned as she ran over to defend her friend.

A big smile formed on George's chubby, round face. "Yeah, like I'm real scared," he laughed while he pretended to tremble. "What's Mrs. *Jerkman* going to do? Call my mommy?"

Katie and Suzanne stared at George in amazement. He'd just called their teacher, Mrs. Derkman, a mean name—and he hadn't even whispered it! He didn't seem scared to have the teacher phone his mom, either.

Before Katie or Suzanne could answer George, Mrs. Derkman blew her red whistle three times.

Phew! Recess was over. It was time to go back to class. Katie was very glad. She used her hands to wipe off some of the mud, and then ran to line up.

"You okay?" Jeremy whispered to Katie.

"I guess," Katie replied.

"George is a creep. You know that."

Katie nodded. But knowing that wasn't going to make George stop calling her the Mud Monster. He'd probably go at it all day, unless . . .

Katie couldn't help wishing that someone else would do something embarrassing that afternoon. Then maybe George Brennan would tease that kid instead.

Chapter 2

"This is for you," Kevin whispered to Katie. He handed her a note. It was written on light-blue paper and folded up really small. Katie knew it was from Suzanne. Her notes always looked like that.

"If you have an answer for her, send it yourself," Kevin told Katie. "I don't want to get into trouble again."

Katie understood. Kevin sat at the desk right between Suzanne and Katie. He always wound up passing notes from girl to girl. Yesterday, Mrs. Derkman had caught Kevin passing a note from Katie to Suzanne. Kevin had had to write an apology note to Mrs. Derkman.

Katie unfolded the paper. *Do you want to come over after school?* the note read.

Katie scribbled her answer on the bottom of the note. *No, thanks. I have to go home and change. Maybe tomorrow?*

Katie tossed the paper over Kevin's head. It landed right on Suzanne's desk. Katie crossed her fingers, hoping Mrs. Derkman didn't see.

Katie lucked out. Mrs. Derkman didn't notice the flying note. She was too busy writing on the board.

"Okay, take out your pencils and math notebooks. Today we're going to review subtraction with borrowing," the teacher announced.

Katie gulped. Whenever Mrs. Derkman said the word "review," it meant that she was going to ask some of the kids in the class to go to the board and solve the problems in front of everyone.

Katie slid down low in her chair, hoping

Mrs. Derkman wouldn't notice her. She didn't want to be one of the kids who were called on. It wasn't that Katie couldn't do subtraction with borrowing. It was more that she hated being in front of the whole class.

"I'll try one, Mrs. Derkman," Suzanne volunteered.

Katie sighed. Suzanne never worried about making a mistake in front of the whole class. She just liked being the center of attention. Katie wished she could be more like that.

But today, Mrs. Derkman didn't ask Suzanne to come up to the board. She picked Mandy Banks, Zoe Canter, and Jeremy instead. Mandy went first. She whizzed through her problem. No surprise there—she was like a computer when it came to math. Next it was Zoe's turn.

"All right, Zoe," Mrs. Derkman said as Zoe walked up to the board. "What will you get when you subtract 152 from 901?"

"The wrong answer!" George joked out loud.

Some kids in the class giggled. Zoe blushed.

Katie thought it was really mean of George to joke around like that. Everyone knew Zoe had a lot of trouble with math.

Mrs. Derkman looked sternly over at George, but she smiled at Zoe. "Go ahead," she said to her. "We'll do it together."

When it was his turn, Jeremy took his time solving the subtraction problem. Katie smiled. That was Jeremy: slow and steady like the tortoise in the story of *The Tortoise and the Hare*.

Sometimes Jeremy's careful slowness could get kind of annoying. But not today. *As long as Jeremy's up there, Mrs. Derkman won't call on me,* Katie thought to herself.

But eventually Jeremy did finish the problem. And he got the right answer . . . as usual.

Mrs. Derkman smiled and wrote another math problem on the board. "Let's do one more," she said.

Katie sunk even lower in her chair. Her lip was practically resting on her desk. But it was no use. Mrs. Derkman saw her anyway.

"Katie, will you solve this for us?" the teacher asked.

Katie sighed. She stood up and slowly walked toward the board.

"Here comes the Mud Monster!" Katie heard George whisper as she walked past his desk. Katie didn't want to walk past George, but she had no choice. He sat right in the front row—where Mrs. Derkman could keep an eye on him.

Katie reached the board and picked up a piece of yellow chalk. She opened her mouth to take a deep, calming breath. But instead of breathing in air, she let out a great big belch.

It was the loudest burp she'd ever heard. A real record-breaker.

The other kids in class began to laugh. Katie blushed beet red. "I'm sorry," she apologized to Mrs. Derkman. Katie didn't want her teacher to think she'd done that on purpose.

Out of the corner of her eye, Katie could see George holding his nose. He was pretending to die from the smell of her breath.

"Katie's stinking up the classroom!" George exclaimed. He laughed so hard, he nearly fell off his chair.

Chapter 3

For the rest of that day, everywhere Katie looked, someone was laughing at her. Mostly because George kept cracking jokes.

"Hey, Mud Monster, can you burp a song for us?" he asked. "I can." George began to belch out the ABC song. By the time he got to Z, the other kids were all giggling.

"Hey, you know something?" George announced. "Burping a song kinda sounds like a kazoo. That's what your name should be, Katie. Not Katie Carew. Katie *Kazoo*!" Then he started chanting, "Katie Kazoo, Katie Kazoo," over and over again.

The other kids began to join in. "Katie

Kazoo. Katie Kazoo. Katie Kazoo. Katie Kazoo!"

Katie sank down in her chair. She tried hard not to cry.

"All right, that's enough," Mrs. Derkman scolded the class. She turned to George. "I'm sending a note home to your mother. I expect you to bring it back to me with her signature."

George shrugged as if he didn't care.

As the afternoon went on, Katie wished the other kids would stop laughing when George teased her. He really wasn't all that funny. But she did kind of understand why the kids kept laughing. If they didn't, George might make fun of them next.

Before school ended, Katie walked over toward the window, where the hamster cage was. It was her turn to feed Speedy this week.

Hamsters are so lucky, Katie thought to herself as she watched Speedy running on his wheel. *They never have bad days. Every day is just the same for them.*

Finally, the bell rang. The day was over. Katie grabbed her books and ran for the door. She had to make sure she was the first one out of the classroom.

But it didn't matter. George caught up to Katie right away. He followed her halfway home. "Katie Kazoo, I see you!" he shouted.

"Hey, Katie, wait up!"

Katie could hear Jeremy calling after her as she ran towards her house. She knew he just wanted to make her feel better. But Katie didn't stop. She didn't want to hang out with Jeremy. She just wanted to get home, go upstairs to her room, and shut the door.

Even that wasn't easy to do. When Katie got home, her mother was sitting on the front steps, waiting for her.

"Hi, Kat!" Her mother greeted her with her special nickname. "I made some yummy chocolate-chip cookies. Want some?"

"I, um, I'm not hungry right now," Katie mumbled. She raced past her and opened the screen door. "I gotta get homework done."

As Katie entered her room, she found her brown-and-white cocker spaniel, Pepper, lying on her bed. Pepper picked up his head and looked at Katie. He reached out his long, pink tongue and gave her a big kiss. Katie hugged her dog tightly.

"Thanks, Pepper," she whispered quietly into his brown floppy ear. "At least *someone* isn't making fun of me today."

Pepper looked up at her and smiled.

Jeremy was always telling Katie that dogs couldn't really smile. But Katie was sure that Pepper could. "Pepper's just a really special dog," she would tell Jeremy when he argued with her. "He's even smarter than people."

Now, as Pepper lay his head in her lap,

Katie decided that even if her cocker spaniel wasn't smarter than people, he certainly was nicer.

That night at dinner, Katie picked at her spaghetti. She rolled the long noodles around on her fork. Then she pushed the meatballs over to the side of her plate and scowled.

Three weeks ago, Katie had told her mother that she was a vegetarian. Her mother kept giving her meat anyway. Well, Katie was just not going to eat the meatballs, that's all.

"You wouldn't believe the day I had at the office," Katie's father announced as he took a bite of his meatball. "We have this new guy, and he was working on the computer when . . ."

Usually Katie hated it when her father took up the whole dinner talking about his accounting firm. But tonight she was happy to sit quietly and let him talk. It was better than having to explain why she was so miserable.

Unfortunately, her dad's story finally came

to an end. Immediately, Katie's mother changed the subject. "So, Kat, what's new with you?" she asked.

Katie shrugged. "Nothing."

"Really?" her mother asked. "Well, you sure had a lot of homework. I haven't seen you since you got home."

Katie nodded slowly. "We had a ton of social studies questions," she muttered. "Um . . . I'm not so hungry. Can I be excused?"

Katie watched as her parents gave each other their "nervous" looks. They knew something was wrong. They just weren't sure what to do about it. Finally, her mother said, "Sure, Kat. Go ahead. I'll clear the table."

Katie stood up and walked out of the room. She opened the front door, and sat on the stoop outside her house. She looked out into the darkness. Suddenly the whole rotten day flashed in front of her eyes.

She thought about missing the football and losing the game for her team.

She thought about her new jeans in the hamper, all caked with mud.

She thought about the belch she'd let out during math.

Worst of all, she thought about what George was going to do to her tomorrow.

"I wish I could be anyone but me!" she shouted out loud.

A shooting star shot across the dark night sky. But Katie was too upset to notice it.

Chapter 4

"Rise and shine, Katie! You're going to be late for school!" Katie's mother called from the kitchen.

Katie sat up slowly and rubbed the sleep from her eyes. She squinted at the Mickey Mouse clock on her wall. Mickey's hands were on the 8 and the 3. Oh no! It was already 8:15. School started at 8:45. She only had half an hour to get dressed, eat breakfast, and walk to school. This day was starting out really lousy.

Her mother had put out Katie's clothes for the day—a bright yellow satiny blouse and black jeans. The outfit was very cheerful.

But Katie wasn't feeling cheerful today. She went to her closet and pulled out a gray sweatshirt and jeans instead. That's how she felt. *Blech*. Like a gray, cloudy day.

As Katie came into the kitchen, her mother noticed her new outfit. "Not in the mood for yellow, huh kiddo?" she asked kindly.

Katie shook her head.

"Did you have an argument with Suzanne or Jeremy?" her mother guessed.

"No," Katie answered.

"So what's wrong?" her mother asked.

Katie thought about telling her mother what had happened yesterday. But she was afraid that her mom would call the school to complain about George's bullying. Imagine how mean George would be to her if *that* happened!

"Nothing's wrong," Katie lied to her mother. "I'm just tired."

Her mom didn't say anything. But Katie could tell she didn't believe her.

"You'd better eat that toast," her mom said. "It's getting late."

Katie nodded and slowly took a nibble of her bread. She slowly chewed each tiny bite until the toast practically melted in her mouth.

Katie *wanted* to be late.

If she arrived after the bell rang, the class would all be seated and doing their work by the time she got there. Mrs. Derkman would be upset that she was late. But it was worth it if she could avoid even a little bit of George's teasing. Definitely.

"You've got to get going," Katie's mother warned her. "You can eat the rest on the way."

Katie didn't say anything. She slipped on her backpack and headed for the door.

"Have a good day, kiddo," her mother called.

By the time Katie finally reached the school, everyone was inside the building. Katie stood outside by her classroom window. She watched as her classmates scrambled into their seats. Katie knew she should hurry inside. But her feet just didn't seem to want to move.

Just then, the wind began to blow. It started out as a slow and gentle breeze. But within seconds the wind was swirling round and

round like a tornado. The weird thing was that the wild wind was only blowing around Katie. The leaves on the trees weren't moving. The bushes weren't moving. Even the flag up on the flagpole wasn't moving.

What was going on? Katie was really scared. She wished she were inside. Away from this wind. She hugged herself tightly, and closed her eyes.

And then, suddenly, everything was calm again. The wind had disappeared as quickly as it had started. Katie stood perfectly still for a moment, waiting to see if it would start up again. Finally, when she was sure the storm was over, Katie slowly opened her eyes.

Everything seemed blurry. Katie blinked really hard. Nothing changed. She still couldn't see very well.

But she could smell *really* well. And her nose was twitching. Katie stood up tall and sniffed at the air. All around her were yucky smells: salami, egg salad, old sneakers. It was hard to tell where each smell was coming from. The scents were all mixing together.

Katie hadn't only become a champion smeller. She could also hear really well. *Too* well, in fact. Everyone in the classroom seemed to be shouting. All the noise was making her nervous. Katie could feel her heart beating really, really fast.

Now Katie was really scared. She wanted to

run right home. But her parents were probably at work by now. There was no one at home to take care of her. If Katie didn't show up at school, Mrs. Derkman would phone her mother for sure. Katie definitely did not want that to happen. She ran towards the classroom. She'd have to hope her sight got better.

Bam! She bashed right into a solid glass wall.

That was weird, Katie thought. *There hadn't been a glass wall there before.*

"What's going on here?" Katie cried out.

Nobody answered. All the kids in the classroom were so busy yelling, they couldn't hear Katie's cries.

"Hello!" Katie shouted. "Can anyone hear me?"

Katie began running wildly in circles. She didn't get very far before she bashed head first into another glass wall. *Ouch!* That one really hurt.

As she reached up to rub her head, Katie

noticed that her hand looked strange. This hand was small and furry. This hand had nails  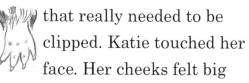 that really needed to be clipped. Katie touched her face. Her cheeks felt big and round like huge empty pouches, and her face was all hairy!

Quickly, Katie looked down at her body.

"Aaah!" she cried out. "I'm naked!"

Actually, she wasn't completely naked. Her back and stomach were covered with orange-brown fur!

And that's when Katie realized what had happened. She wasn't outside anymore. She was inside—in a hamster cage. She'd become Speedy, the class hamster.

Katie tried to scream, but the only sound that came out of her mouth was a loud squeak.

Chapter 5

"Hey, look at Speedy!" Zoe Canter called out from the other side of the glass. "He's going crazy!"

Within seconds, eighteen pairs of giant eyes were peering through the glass window. They were all staring at Katie.

Katie was really confused. How could this have happened? It didn't make any sense. People didn't just turn into hamsters.

Then Katie remembered. She'd made that wish the night before. She'd said she wanted to be anyone but herself!

"Why did *this* have to be my first wish to come true?" Katie yelped. (Of course, to the kids in class 3A, her words sounded more like "Squeak, squeak squeak, squeak squeak!")

"Somebody should throw some oil on that hamster!" George exclaimed. "That'll stop his squeaking."

"Oh, George, be quiet," Suzanne told him. "Something is obviously bothering the little guy. We should try and help him."

"It figures a rat would want to help a hamster," George said. "You're both in the same family."

"Cut it out," Suzanne replied.

"Hey, Ratgirl, show us your tail," George teased.

Katie wished she could help Suzanne, but she was just a little hamster. Luckily, George had to stop when Mrs. Derkman told them all to sit back down.

"I've got to get out of this cage," Katie squeaked to herself.

The problem was that she knew there wasn't any way out. The only opening in the cage

was at the top, and that was covered by a
screened lid. The lid was Mrs. Derkman's way
of making sure Speedy didn't escape. Now the
lid was making sure Katie didn't escape, either.

There had to be some way to get that lid off. Katie might have a hamster body now, but she still had a human brain. She was smart enough to get out of a hamster cage. She just had to come up with a plan.

Before she could think about anything, though, she had to deal with her teeth. They were feeling really long. She needed to chew on something—and fast! Quickly, Katie scampered over to a small pile of brightly colored pieces of wood.

"Ahh, that feels better." Katie sighed as she bit into a bright green chew stick. She could feel her teeth getting shorter with each nibble.

Suddenly Katie had an idea. She took the green chew stick in her mouth and placed it on top of a yellow one. Then she grabbed a blue stick and placed it on top of the green one.

If I can just build this high enough, maybe I can climb up and push the lid off, Katie thought to herself, as she took an orange chew stick and added it to the pile.

It took a while, but at last Katie built what had to be the biggest chew-stick ladder of all time. (It also was probably the *only* chew-stick ladder of all time!) If Katie could climb to the top of the pile, she might be able to reach the lid.

"Hey, look what Speedy made," she heard Manny Gonzalez whisper to Kevin.

"Cool!" Kevin agreed. "It's like a chew-stick mountain."

Katie licked her little front paws and admired her work. She took a deep breath. It was time to try out her plan. Carefully, Katie stepped onto the bottom chew stick. *So far so good,* she thought.

Once Katie was safely on the first rung of the ladder, she stood tall on her hind legs and tried to pull herself up to the next rung.

Bonk! The entire pile of chew sticks came crashing down on top of Katie's head. Luckily, the sticks were made of a soft wood. Katie wasn't hurt. And it was kind of fun eating her way out of the pile of chew sticks.

"I have to stop this!" Katie said to herself as she chewed. "I'll never get out of here if I don't stop thinking like a hamster."

The trouble was, Katie *was* a hamster. And right then she suddenly couldn't think about anything but Speedy's hamster wheel. Katie couldn't explain why she suddenly needed to run so badly. She just did. She couldn't help herself.

"Hey, this is fun," Katie squealed as her tiny paws moved faster and faster inside the wheel.

The wheel squeaked very loudly as Katie ran. The noise didn't bother Katie's sensitive hamster ears. In fact, she kind of liked it. Mrs. Derkman, on the other hand, didn't like the squeaking at all.

"Suzanne, will you please put a carrot in Speedy's cage?" Mrs. Derkman asked. "Maybe that will get him to stop running on that squeaky wheel."

"Yes, Mrs. Derkman," Suzanne said.

Katie watched as her best friend walked over, lifted the lid off the cage, and dropped in a carrot.

Katie leaped from the wheel and grabbed the treat. As she chewed the carrot, Katie looked up gratefully at Suzanne. Her friend had given Katie more than just a snack. She'd given her a great idea, too!

Chapter 6

Katie dropped the carrot and raced over to Speedy's wheel. She started running as fast as her tiny hamster feet could carry her. The wheel moved round and round. The squeaking got louder and louder.

"Excuse me, class," Mrs. Derkman said finally. "I'm going to have to take Speedy's wheel out of his cage. The noise is making it too hard to learn."

Katie heard Mrs. Derkman's footsteps come near the glass cage. Her tiny hamster heart beat quickly. This was her only chance to get free!

Mrs. Derkman took the lid from the cage.

She reached in with her hand and tried to gently ease the hamster off the wheel.

Before Mrs. Derkman could push her off, Katie leaped out and raced up her teacher's arm. Mrs. Derkman jumped back with surprise as the furry little creature scurried over her bare skin.

Katie looked from Mrs. Derkman's elbow to the floor below. It seemed very far away. But Katie knew she had no choice. She placed her little hamster paws in front of her eyes and jumped!

Thump! Katie landed hard on the cold tile floor. Her hind legs hurt a little. So did her ears. Everyone in the class seemed to be moving and shouting at once.

"Speedy's loose!" Kevin announced.

"Somebody catch him!" Zoe shouted.

"I'll get him," Jeremy volunteered. He got down on his hands and knees.

"No, I'll do it," Ricky Dobbs said. He got down on his hands and knees, too.

"I think I can get him," Mandy yelled.

Suddenly everyone seemed to be grabbing for Katie. Her little hamster body shook with fear. She was lost in a big pile of giant human hands. They were all grabbing for her. Katie couldn't let the kids catch her. They'd put her back in the cage again!

Katie ran toward the front of the room. It seemed more empty there. But as she reached Mrs. Derkman's desk, she caught a whiff of human. Whoever was standing there was covered in kid smells—spilled orange juice, crumbs, and waxy crayons.

Suddenly, the boy by the desk shrieked. "Get it away from me! Get this thing away from me!"

Katie would know that voice anywhere. It was George. She couldn't believe it! The big class bully was scared of a tiny little hamster.

Katie couldn't help herself. She ran over to George and brushed up against his leg. Then she climbed right over his shoe.

"AAAAH!" George screamed as he leaped up onto Mrs. Derkman's desk. He stood there, high off the ground, shaking. "Get it! Somebody catch that furball!" he screamed.

Katie laughed to herself. The class bully had been bullied—by a tiny little hamster. Deep down, Katie knew she'd been pretty mean. Her parents had always told her that two wrongs don't make a right, but Katie couldn't help feeling just a little bit happy at hearing George screaming in fear.

Just then, the classroom door opened.

Mr. Kane, the principal, was standing at the door. "What's going on in here?" he asked.

"Our hamster is loose," Suzanne explained quickly.

"There he goes!" Miriam added, as Katie ran right between Mr. Kane's legs and out the door.

"Hang on, Speedy!" Kevin cried out. "We'll save you!"

Chapter 7

"Not so fast, Kevin," Mr. Kane said. "I can't have a whole third-grade class running around the school."

"But we have to find Speedy," Kevin argued.

"Right now you have to go to gym class," Mrs. Derkman interrupted. "I'm sure Speedy will turn up."

"But Mrs. Derkman," Jeremy pleaded. "He could get stuck in a wall or something."

Mrs. Derkman sighed. "I'm sure he'll be fine, Jeremy. Now, class, let's line up. We're already late."

⌗ ⌗ ⌗

Katie raced down the hall as quickly as her little legs could take her. She was looking for someplace where she could be safe.

As she turned the corner, Katie found herself in a small empty room. What a relief! There was no one here to chase her. She stood on her hind legs and began to clean her front paws with her little pink tongue.

Just then, Katie heard footsteps coming into the room. She froze in place as someone turned on a light.

"Man, Brennan, you are such a chicken!" Katie recognized Ricky's voice. "I didn't think you would be afraid of a tiny hamster."

"I'm not," George answered him.

"So how come you were screaming like that?" Ricky continued.

"How come your face is like that?" George argued back.

It wasn't much of an answer, but it sure shut Ricky up. "I'm not afraid of anything," George continued.

Katie sniffed at the air. The room was beginning to smell like old sneakers and dirty socks.

"Do you think Coach G. will make us play kickball again?" Kevin asked. "I hate that game."

"Well, we'd better hurry up and get out there. Coach gets mad when we take too long in the locker room," Jeremy said.

Katie's eyes grew wide. Oh no! She was in the boys' locker room . . . while the boys were getting dressed for gym! This was so embarrassing!

Katie had to find a good hiding place.

Someplace where the boys couldn't see her.

Someplace where she couldn't see anything she wasn't supposed to see!

Quickly, Katie leaped into the nearest small hole. She landed in some sort of strange, soft cave. She crept inside as far as she could go. Then she sat very, very still.

The inside of the cave was moist and

stinky. It smelled like sweaty feet. But at least it was dark and quiet. No one would find her here.

Suddenly, Katie felt someone lift her hiding place right off the floor. Katie peeked out and looked up. A giant, stinky gym sock was coming right at her!

Yikes!

Katie's safe 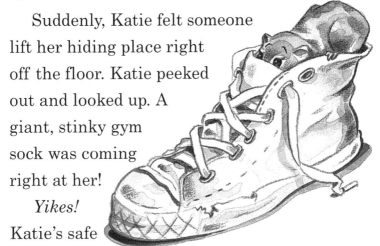 cave was actually someone's sneaker. And whoever the sneaker belonged to was about to crush her with his big, smelly foot!

Katie had to escape from her sneaker cave. She ran toward the opening, and leaped out onto the floor.

"AAAAHHHH!" George screamed as he dropped his sneaker. "There's a mouse in my shoe!" He leaped up on a bench. "Get it out of here!"

"That's no mouse," Ricky yelled. "That's Speedy!"

"We've got to get him," Manny Gonzalez shouted.

But Katie wasn't about to be caught in the boys' locker room. She ran for the door.

¤ ¤ ¤

The boys' screams were way in the distance by the time Katie felt safe enough to stop running. She hid behind a trash can and stood very, very still. She was trying to hear if anyone was coming after her. Luckily, the hallway was silent.

Suddenly a wind began to blow. Katie lifted her little hamster nose and tried to sniff at the breeze. She didn't smell anything unusual— just the ammonia that the janitor, Mr. Peterson, used to clean the floor. She couldn't smell any flowers, trees, or even car fumes coming from outside the school. In fact, there didn't seem to be a window open anywhere.

Still, the wind was definitely blowing. Katie could feel it whipping through her thick, orange fur. It swirled all around her like a tornado . . . exactly as it had just before Katie had turned into a hamster!

Oh no! Katie thought. *What's happening to me now?*

Chapter 8

Finally, the magical wind stopped blowing. But Katie was afraid to open her eyes. She'd already been turned into a hamster. What if this time she were something even worse— like an ant or something?

Slowly, Katie cracked open one eye. She raised her hands to her face. No fur. Good. And she had fingers—five of them on each hand. She looked at her nails. They were filed short. A few of them still showed a few chips of leftover glow-in-the-dark glitter nail polish. These were definitely her hands.

Was it possible? Had she turned back into herself?

Quickly, Katie ran into the girls' room and looked in the mirror. An eight-year-old girl with red hair, green eyes, and a line of freckles across her nose looked back at her. It was true! Katie was back!

Out of the corner of her eye, Katie saw a small orange ball of fluff rush past her into

one of the bathroom stalls. Speedy! The real Speedy was really on the loose. Quickly she ran into the stall. She found Speedy hiding behind the toilet. He seemed frightened and confused.

Katie scooped the hamster up and held him in her hands. "It's okay, little guy," she told him quietly. "Everything's back to normal now."

As Katie walked back to the gym, the voices of her friends became louder. They were all complaining because Coach G. and Mrs. Derkman wouldn't let them chase after Speedy. Katie grinned as she opened the gym door. She would be a hero for bringing the hamster back.

"Were you guys looking for this?" she asked as she walked in the door.

"Katie, where'd you find him?" Suzanne shouted from the other side of the room.

"Oh, we just sort of ran into each other in the girls' room," Katie replied.

"Boy, it was a good thing you were late today," Kevin told her. "Otherwise Speedy might have been gone forever."

"It's never a good thing to be late for school, Kevin," Mrs. Derkman reminded him. "But I am glad you found the hamster, Katie. Now, please take him back to the classroom and put him in his cage. And make sure the lid is on tightly."

Katie did as she was told. She pet Speedy gently as she placed him down on his cage floor. Then she handed him a treat bar.

"You deserve this," she whispered quietly. "We worked really hard this morning."

Speedy slept for the rest of the morning. Katie spent the time trying to keep her mind on her lessons. But it was hard for her to think about anything other than her adventure. After all, how often does an eight-year-old girl turn into a hamster?

Katie wished she could tell Jeremy and Suzanne all about what had happened to her. But she knew they would never believe her. She wouldn't believe it either if it hadn't happened to her.

This was one secret Katie would have to keep to herself.

"Boy, did you pick the wrong morning to be late," Jeremy told Katie as they walked out onto the playground after lunch. "It was so weird. Speedy was out of his mind. I'd never seen him like that!"

"I'd never seen George like that either," Suzanne giggled. "I can't believe you missed it, Katie. He was terrified of a little hamster. What a wimp!"

"I can't believe we were ever scared of

George," Miriam agreed.

"I was never afraid of him," Kevin argued.

Jeremy rolled his eyes. "So how come you walk three blocks out of your way to get to school—just so you don't have to pass his house on the way?"

Kevin blushed.

The kids looked over at George. He was sitting on a bench all by himself. He didn't look mean anymore. He just looked lonely.

"Hey, George!" Manny Gonzalez called out. "Why did the hamster cross the road?"

George didn't answer. He obviously didn't want to talk about hamsters.

"Because it was the chicken's day off!" Manny finished off his own joke. Then he waited for George to say something mean to him.

But George didn't say anything. He just scowled and turned away. For the first time, the other kids were doing the teasing. George didn't like that at all.

"Well, I guess we don't have to be afraid of George anymore," Jeremy said to the others.

Suzanne nodded. "We have Speedy to thank for that."

Katie smiled to herself. She knew that class 3A actually had her to thank for stopping George's bullying. She was a real hero.

Chapter 9

Katie was in a great mood when she got home that afternoon. Pepper met her at the steps. Katie bent down and gave her cocker spaniel a huge hug.

Pepper licked her on the nose.

"Well, I'm glad to see you're happy again," Katie's mother said as she came out of the house with two glasses of pink lemonade. "You just weren't yourself this morning."

Katie laughed. Her mother didn't know the half of it.

"So, did anything exciting happen at school today?" her mother asked.

Katie almost choked on her lemonade. It

was only the most exciting—and scary—day of her whole life! But Katie couldn't tell her mother that. Instead she said, "Our hamster got loose, and I caught him!"

"Good for you!" her mother said. Then she shuddered. "I can't imagine having a hamster running loose around a classroom. I don't really like little rodents like that."

"Oh, you'd like Speedy, Mom. I know you would." Katie finished off her drink.

"So, what do you want to do this afternoon?" Katie's mom asked as she sipped slowly at her drink. "You want to come inside and have some cookies before you start your homework?"

Katie shook her head. "We don't have a whole lot of homework today. Just a current events worksheet. So can Pepper and I go for a walk?"

"I don't see why not," her mother said. "You can do the worksheet after dinner. I'll put the newspaper up in your room."

Katie handed her mom the empty glass and jumped up.

"Come on, Pepper!" she called out. "Let's walk!"

Katie never thought she'd be so happy just to walk around on two legs. But it felt great to stand straight and tall. She loved being able to run wherever she wanted, not just on some silly, squeaky wheel. Katie did a big cartwheel, right in the middle of the sidewalk.

Unfortunately, Katie was not very good at cartwheels. Instead of landing on her feet, she landed— *splat*—right on her rear end.

As Katie stood

up, she noticed a boy about her age sitting alone on his front porch. He was wearing dark sunglasses and a baseball hat. At first she didn't recognize him. Then the boy called out, "You okay?"

It was George Brennan. A nervous feeling came over Katie. Was George going to make fun of her for falling down?

"I said, are you okay?"

Katie stood up and brushed off her jeans. "Yeah, I'm fine. Thanks." She looked at George. He seemed more embarrassed than she was. He seemed kind of sad, too.

For the first time, Katie felt a little sorry for George. At least when George had made fun of her for falling in the mud, she'd had friends to cheer her up. George had no one.

"Is this your house?" she asked him nervously.

"No, I just like to sit on other people's porches," George snapped back, making a nasty joke. "Of course it's my house."

Katie turned and began to walk away. If George was going to be mean, she wasn't going to talk to him.

"Hey, is that your dog?" George called after her.

Katie stopped walking. She turned around and smiled. "No, I just like hanging out with other people's dogs," she joked back. "Of course he's my dog."

George smiled—a little bit. "Good one," he admitted.

Katie smiled back. "His name's Pepper. You want to pet him? Or are you afraid of dogs, too?"

George blushed. "Never mind."

Katie felt bad. She hadn't been teasing. She really didn't know if George had a problem with all animals, or just hamsters.

"No, I mean it," she assured him. "If you were afraid of dogs, it wouldn't be such a bad thing. A lot of people are afraid dogs will bite or something. But Pepper wouldn't do that."

"I'm not afraid of dogs," George told her. "I'm not even afraid of hamsters. This morning I was just sort of goofing on all the kids who were afraid of Speedy. You weren't there. You should have seen them all crying and screaming and stuff."

Katie knew that was a lie. None of the other kids were afraid of Speedy. They were all trying to catch the hamster. The only kid crying and jumping on chairs was George.

But Katie didn't tell George that. He'd only wonder how she knew what was going on in the classroom, since the whole class thought she was late for school today. Besides, George must have felt really embarrassed about being afraid of hamsters. Why else would he lie about it?

"Oh, I guess everyone else got it wrong," Katie told him, trying to be nice.

"I guess," George mumbled.

"So, you want to pet my dog then?" Katie asked.

"Okay," George said quietly.

Katie walked Pepper up toward George's house. George reached his hand out slowly. It was obvious that he was nervous around dogs, too, but he wasn't going to admit it to Katie. Pepper sat on his hind legs and lifted his head. When George gave Pepper a little pat, the dog licked George's hand. George wrinkled up his nose. He wasn't used to dog kisses.

"He's a pretty cool dog," George admitted.

"Thanks," Katie replied, sitting down next to George. "You know, it's okay to be afraid of something."

George frowned. "Oh yeah, right. So what are you afraid of?"

"I *was* afraid of you—at least until today," Katie admitted.

George smiled. He seemed almost proud of the fact that Katie had been scared of him.

"So you're not afraid of me anymore, huh?" he asked her finally.

Katie shook her head. "Nope."

"I guess none of the kids are scared of me after today," George moaned.

"Why would you want us to be scared of you?" Katie asked.

George shrugged. "Just because."

"I don't know why you have to make mean jokes all the time," Katie said.

"I make jokes so that people will laugh," George told her. "I'd rather have people laugh

at my jokes than laugh at me."

"Why do you think people will laugh at you?" Katie asked him.

George looked at her and rolled his eyes. "Are you kidding? I'm the new kid. Everyone makes fun of the new kid. They laugh at the way the new kid talks, and the clothes the new kid wears. This is the third school I've been to since kindergarten. My dad has had to switch jobs three times. But you know what? After today, I wish my family could move again."

"Don't say that!" Katie exclaimed. "Don't make wishes you don't really mean. You never know when they'll come true."

"But I'm miserable here," George said. "All the kids hate me. And now they won't even laugh at my jokes."

Katie thought about that for a minute. Then she had an idea. "Don't you know any jokes that aren't mean?" Katie asked George. "You can still make kids laugh without making them feel bad."

"I don't know," George answered. "I've never thought about jokes that weren't mean."

"I have a bunch of joke books at my house. Do you want to come over and look at some of them? You can try the jokes out on the kids at school tomorrow."

George didn't say anything at first. Then he looked sort of embarrassed. "I'm sorry I kept calling you Katie Kazoo," he said finally.

Katie grinned. "It's okay. I kind of like it, actually."

"You do?" George asked.

Katie nodded. "It's a pretty cool nickname. It's the kind of name Suzanne would give herself—if she could."

George looked at Katie. "How come you're being nice to me?" he demanded.

Katie shrugged. "I guess because you're being nice to me," she said simply.

Chapter 10

The next morning Katie was up and dressed before her parents awoke. She wanted to be sure to get to school before George did. Katie had a feeling that the other kids were going to make fun of George for being afraid of Speedy. If they did, he might be mean right back to them. Then he would never make friends at school.

Katie really wanted to help George. They had spent a lot of time laughing at joke books together yesterday afternoon. George was really an okay kid. Katie hoped the other kids could see that side of him.

Besides, Katie figured that if George made

friends with the kids at school, he wouldn't want to make fun of them. School would be a lot more fun if everybody wasn't always afraid that George would say something mean to them. So, by helping George, Katie was helping all the other kids, too.

If her plan worked, Katie would be a hero two days in a row!

Katie got to the schoolyard ten minutes early. She sat down on a bench and waited for her friends—and George—to arrive.

"You're here early," Suzanne said a few minutes later, plopping down onto the bench beside Katie.

The key chains on Suzanne's backpack jingled and jangled as the pack hit the ground. Suzanne had a stretchy-alien key chain, a Slinky dog key chain, a key chain that looked like a Barbie doll, and key chains from Vermont, Texas, and California. She even had a key chain with a mirror on it.

Katie only had two key chains on her back-pack. One was a photo frame with a picture of Pepper in it. The other one was a little rubber monkey that bounced up and down when you shook it.

"Are you trying to make up for being late yesterday?" Suzanne asked.

Katie shook her head. "I'm just waiting."

"For what?"

Katie shrugged. "Oh, nothing. "

By now Jeremy and Kevin were there, too. Miriam's mother pulled up in her car. Miriam and Mandy leaped out of the backseat. Manny rode up on his bicycle. He locked the ten-speeder to the bike rack and walked over toward the other kids.

Katie looked around. Most of the kids in her class were there. Now she just had to wait for George.

Katie glanced at her watch. School was starting in five minutes. What if George was afraid to show up? The other kids would be sure he was absent because of Speedy. They'd never let him live that down.

Finally, she saw George walking up the hill toward the schoolyard. He was walking very slowly, but he was definitely coming.

"How come you're so late, George?" Katie asked as George joined the group.

"My clock was slow," George replied. "You'd be slow too, if you'd been running all night."

Katie and George looked at each other nervously.

And then the worst thing happened. Nobody laughed. NOBODY. The kids just stood there staring at George.

George blushed red. He looked angrily at Katie.

Katie gulped. This was not good.

Quickly, Katie tried to get George to tell another joke. A funnier one this time.

"Don't you wish this was the last day of school, George?" she asked him.

The kids all stared at Katie. Why was she being so nice to George Brennan?

"You know, Katie, there is one school you have to drop out of before you can graduate," George began.

"What school is that?" Katie asked.

"Parachute school," George told her.

Again, nobody laughed. Now Katie was getting really worried.

And then, out of nowhere, Jeremy started

laughing—really hard. He was totally cracking up. The other kids looked at him in amazement.

Jeremy stared back at them. "What?" he asked. "It was funny."

"Thanks," George said. He sounded a little happier now.

"Tell another one," Katie urged.

"Okay," George agreed. "What's the most important subject a witch learns in school?"

"What?" Katie asked.

"Spelling!" George answered.

Jeremy started laughing again. So did Suzanne. Suddenly all the kids were giggling at George's joke.

"That was a good one," Kevin said. "Got any more jokes?"

George's face broke into a smile. A real, happy smile, not the mean smile he usually had on his face. "Sure, I've got a million of 'em." He looked around at the other kids. "Why didn't the skeleton do well in school?"

"Why?" Suzanne asked.

"Because his heart wasn't in it!" George said.

Everyone started laughing all over again.

"Wait, wait! Here's another one!" George announced. "What's the hardest part about taking a test?"

"What?" asked Mandy.

"The answers!" George told her.

George was on a roll. He couldn't stop telling jokes. That was a good thing, since the kids didn't want him to stop. "What table doesn't have any legs?" he asked Jeremy.

Jeremy thought for a minute, but he couldn't guess. "I don't know," he said finally.

"A multiplication table!" George shouted out.

Once again the kids all started giggling.

Just then, Mrs. Derkman blew her whistle. "Line up, class 3A!" she called out. The kids ran to line up. Katie found herself standing right in front of George. Just one day ago, that would have been an awful place to stand.

But now, Katie didn't mind standing near George at all.

"Hey, Katie Kazoo, what do you have for lunch?" George whispered into Katie's ear.

"I'm going to buy something from the cafeteria," she whispered back. "My mom gave me lunch money today."

"I have peanut butter and Marshmallow Fluff," George said. "My mom hardly ever gives me lunch money."

"You're lucky," Katie said. "The food in the cafeteria stinks. I'd much rather have peanut butter and Marshmallow Fluff."

"We could sit together in the cafeteria and share," George suggested. "I'll give you half of my sandwich if you'll give me half of your dessert."

Katie grinned. "It's a deal!"

As class 3A walked toward the school building, Katie felt a cool breeze blow through her hair. She got a scared feeling in the pit of her stomach. Was this the same wind that had turned her into a hamster yesterday? What was going to happen to her now?

Then Katie noticed that everyone else's hair was blowing around too. This wasn't some sort of magic wind. It was just a normal, everyday breeze—the kind that cools you down without turning you into someone else.

Still, Katie had a feeling she hadn't seen the last of the magic wind. It was bound to start blowing again sometime. So the only question was . . . who was she going to turn into next?

Fun Facts About Hamsters!

If you're like Katie and have a hamster in your classroom, here are some fun facts about your furry friend.

Did you know that:

Hamsters need glasses? Hamsters are very near-sighted. Depending on the breed, they can usually see only a few inches or a few feet in front of themselves.

Hamster teeth never stop growing? They just keep getting longer and longer—unless you give your hamster something to gnaw on, like a wooden chew stick. When hamsters chew, they keep their teeth short and healthy.

Hamsters need lots of exercise? In the wild, hamsters may travel several miles a night in search of food. Hamsters that are kept as pets need the same amount of exercise, which is why they run on their wheels.

Hamsters squeak to get your attention?

Hamsters usually make squeaking noises when they want more food or attention.

Hamsters sometimes eat their poop? As gross as it may sound, hamsters sometimes do just that. Their digestive systems are different than ours. Some hamster poop contains certain nutrients that the hamster needs.

Hamsters don't need shampoo? All hamsters know how to clean themselves. They don't need fancy sponges and shampoo to do it either. Hamsters groom themselves by licking their coat at the back and the front. They also lick their paws and then rub their paws over their face and behind their ears. They do that because they can't actually lick their faces.

Some hamsters take baths in dry sand? Hamsters love rolling around in sand. The sand takes some of the grease off of their skin. That makes them feel more comfortable. If you have a hamster, you might want to put a dish of sand in the cage for the hamster to roll around in.